Fairy Tale Theater
THE UGLY DUCKLING
Illustrations by: CARME PERIS
Adapted by: MÓNICA BOSOM

CHARACTERS:
Narrator, Mother Duck, Ducklings, the Ugly Duckling, First Hen, Turkey, Rooster, Geese, Old Lady, Second Hen, Swans, First Boy, Second Boy, Girl

Narrator:
>Once upon a time there was a mother duck who was hatching six eggs. It was summer, when the grass was very green and the corn was very yellow. The first five ducklings came out of their shells quite soon, but the sixth did not want to come out.

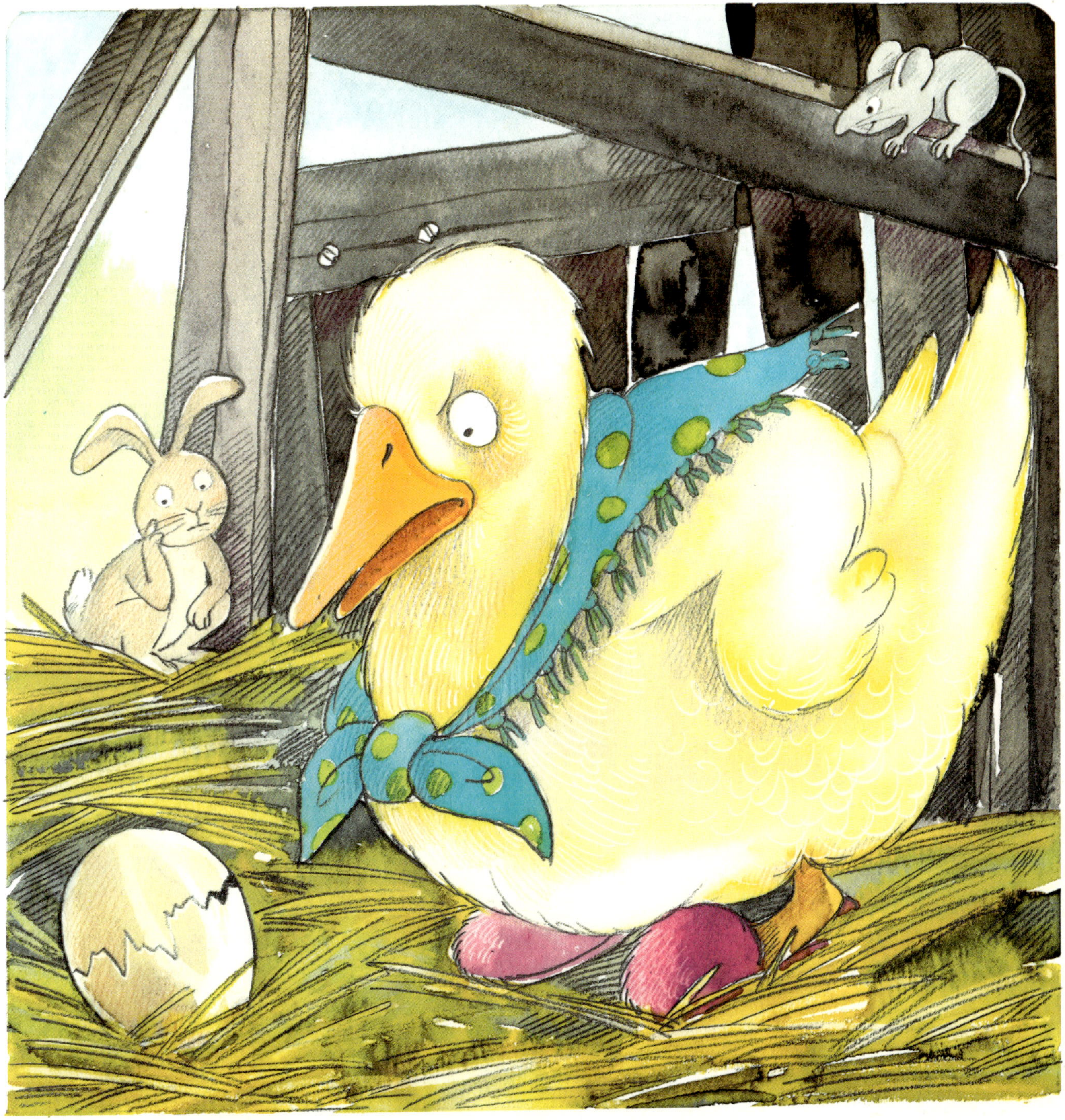

Mother Duck: *(Impatiently)*

"Come on, hurry up, I have hatched you long enough. Get out of there! *(Finally, the eggshell breaks and a different-looking duckling comes out.)* What is that? What an ugly thing! This must be a joke! Someone must have changed one of my eggs for this one. Soon we will know. If it does not want to go into the water, I'll know it's not a duck."

Ducklings:

"Mother, Mother, we want to go swimming in the pond." *(They all go into the water, including the Ugly Duckling.)*

Mother Duck:

"It certainly is not a chicken. It moves its legs like a duck and it looks proud. All things considered, it is not really so ugly. Now we will go visit our neighbors on the farm. Come, I will introduce you to the rest of the animals. And you *(addressing the Ugly Duckling)*, get in the back and try not to be noticed."

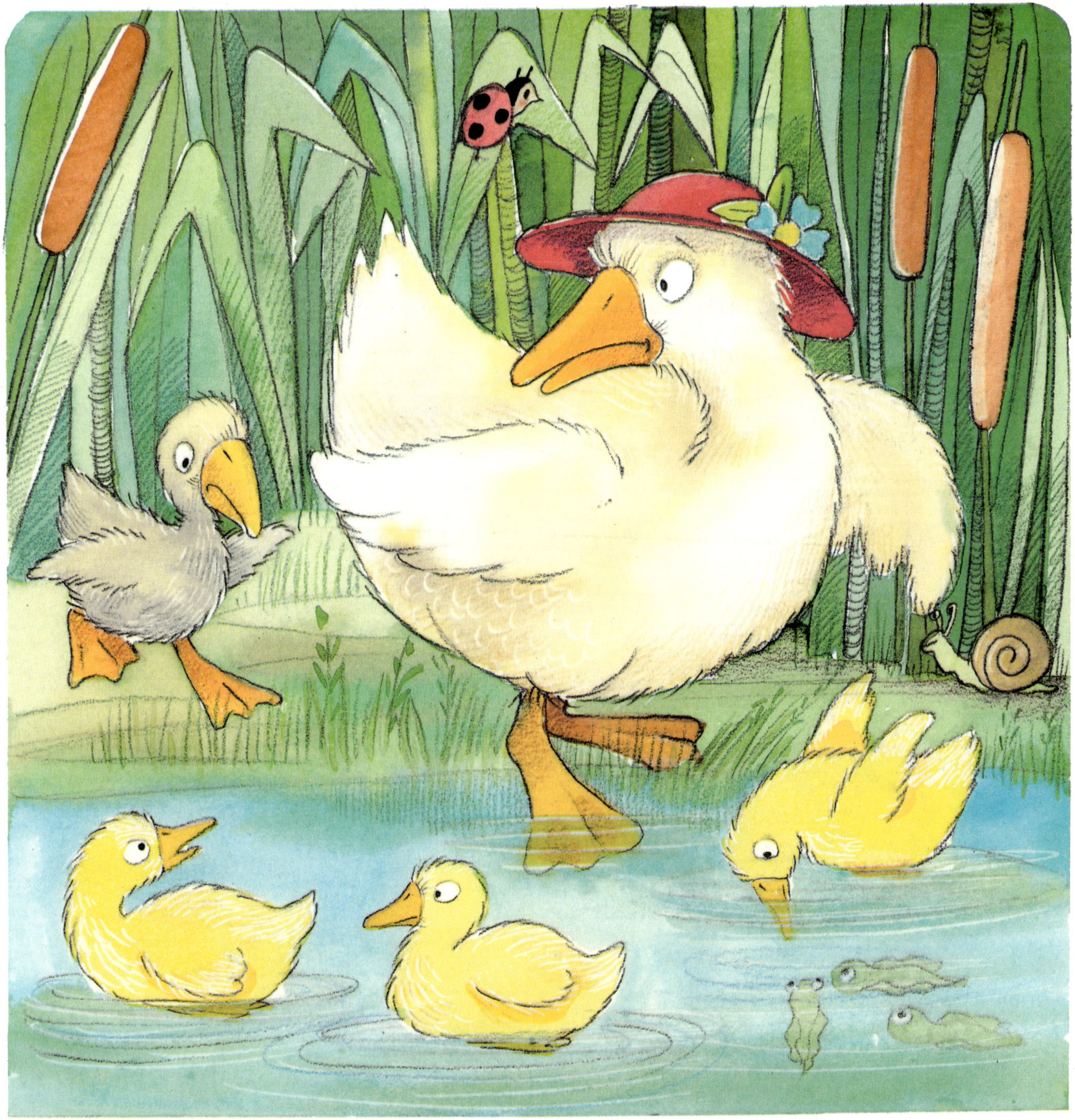

First Hen: *(She sees the Ugly Duckling.)*
"Mother Duck, what an ugly color your duckling is. It is gray, not yellow like the others."

Turkey:
"And it has such long legs."

Rooster:
"Look at the hairs on its head! They are stiff and they stick out! Ha, ha, ha!" *(He laughs very loud and makes the others laugh too.)*

Ugly Duckling: *(Talking to himself)*
"I am so unhappy. Everybody laughs at me. Even the farmer's wife, when she brings us food, kicks me aside with her foot. If only I could fly over the fence... Now—Mother is not looking—it's my chance."

Narrator:
The duckling flies away and spends days and even months hidden among the weeds in a pond. One day, when the sun is shining brightly, it meets some wild geese.

Geese:
"Hey! Look at that ugly thing there in front of us. You poor, lonely thing. Would you like to come with us to the pond? *(Suddenly, some shots are heard. The geese fly away in a hurry.)* The hunters! Hurry! We are in danger!"

Narrator:
As soon as the geese are gone, a dog appears, with its tongue hanging out and its eyes sparkling with excitement. It smells the duckling but then goes on its way.

Ugly Duckling:
"I am so ugly that not even a dog wants to eat me."

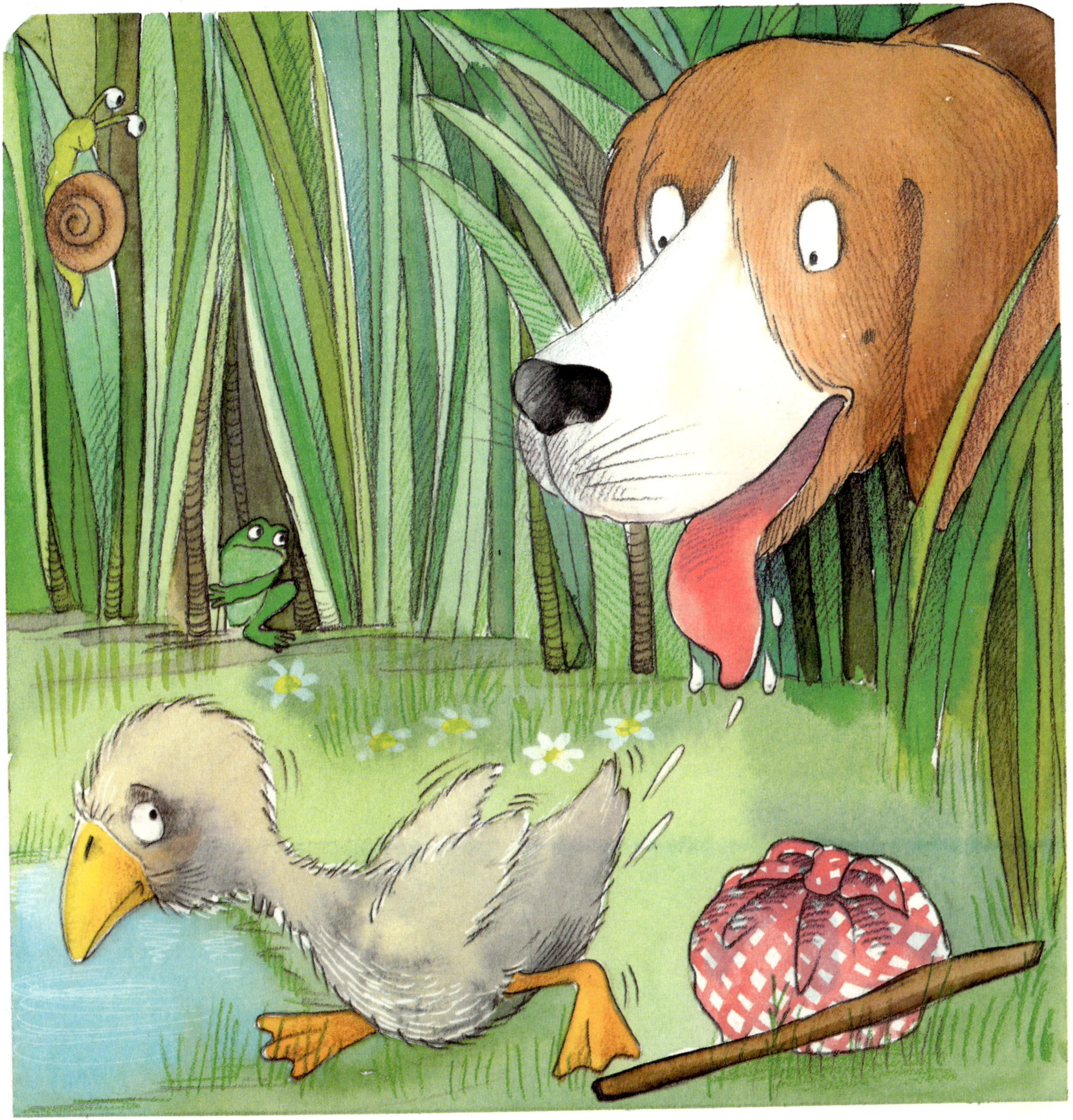

Narrator:
The duckling leaves the pond and finds a little house where there is an old lady, a cat, and a hen.

Old Lady:
"Oh, it is a little duck! It looks like it has not eaten for a long time. I will feed it something, although it really looks strange."

Cat and Second Hen: *(Angry and addressing the Ugly Duckling)* "Do not think you are welcome here just because the old lady has fed you. There is no place for you here. You cannot chase mice and you cannot lay eggs. As soon as you finish eating, you must go."

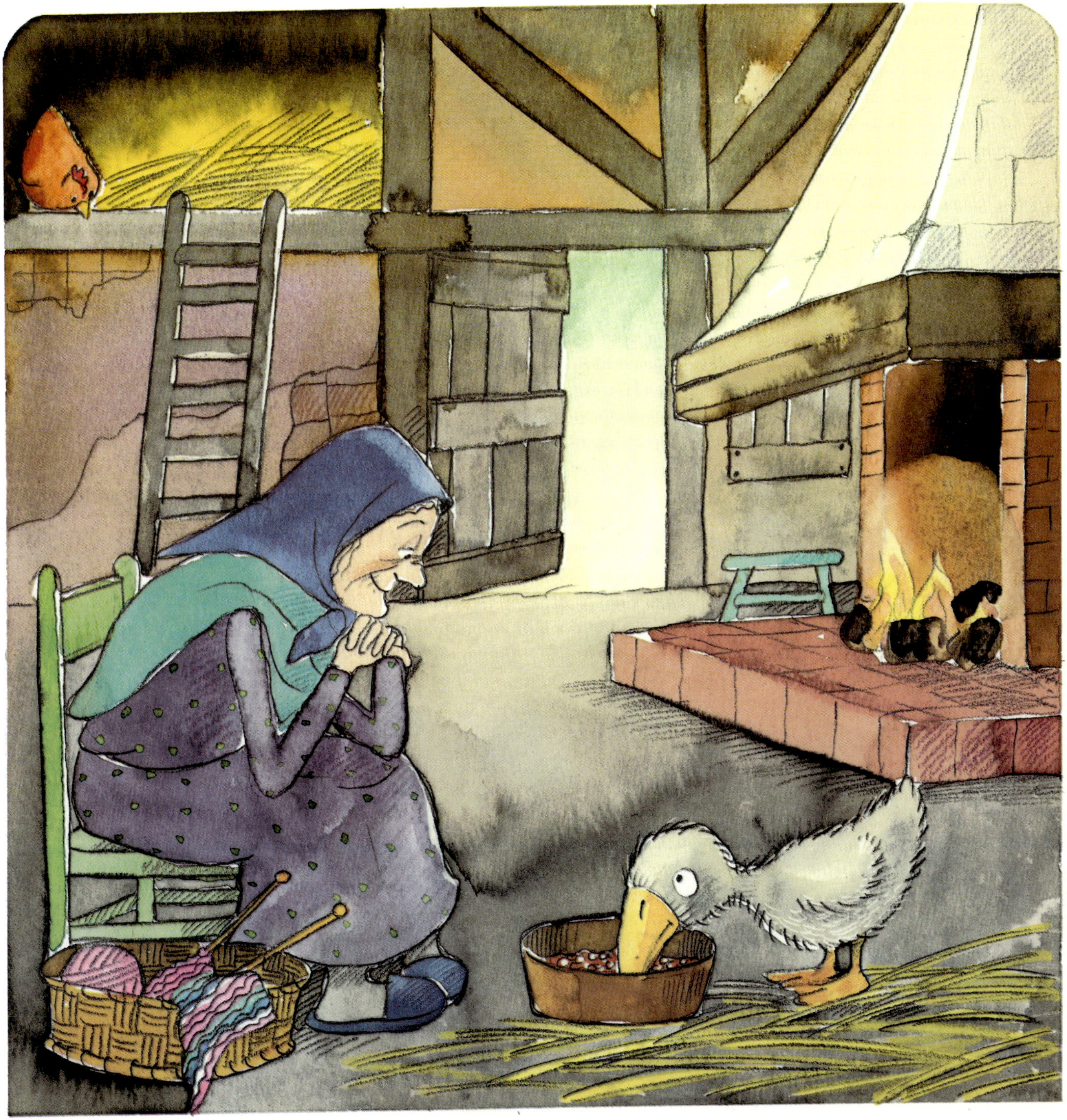

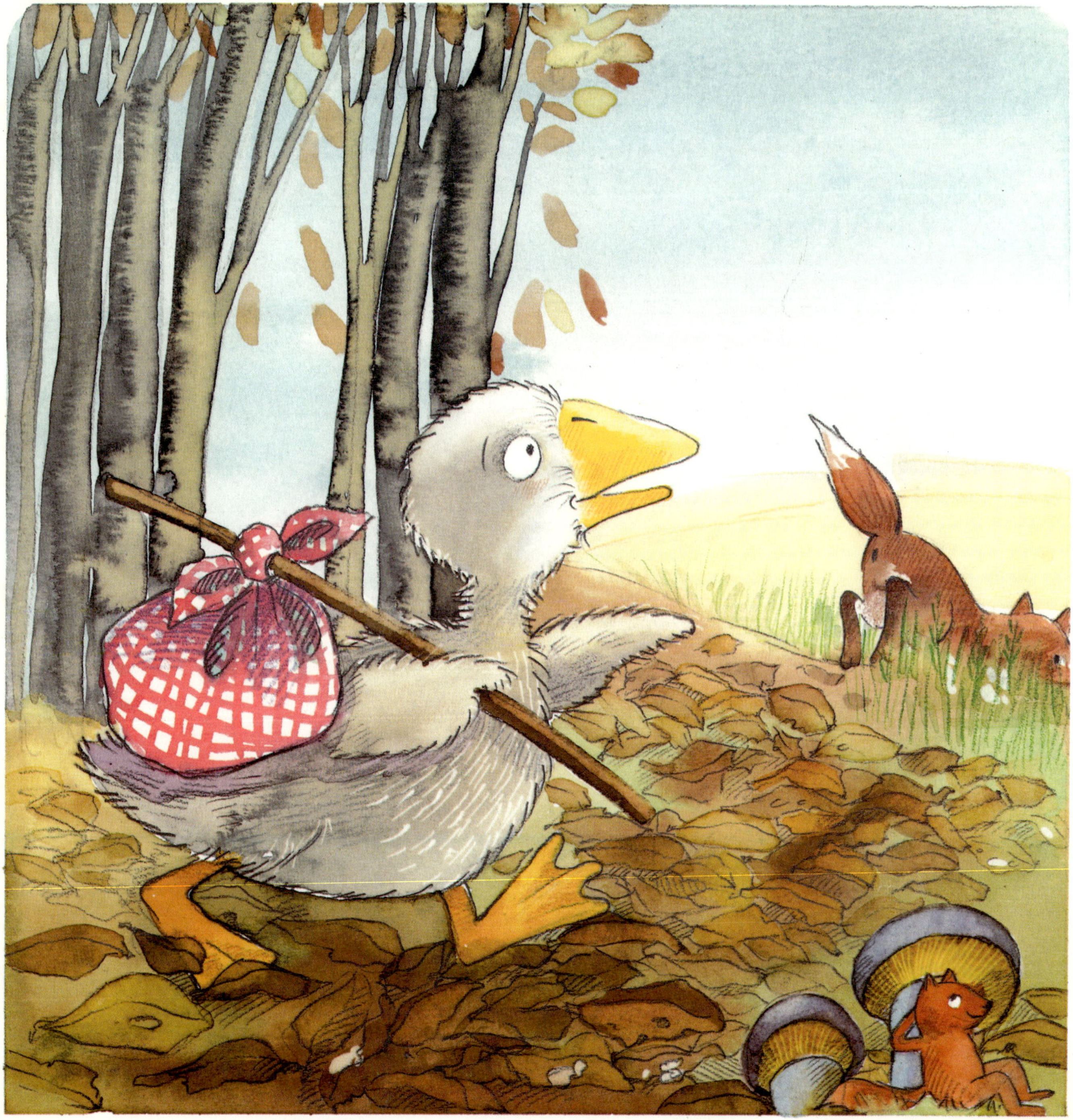

Narrator:
> The Ugly Duckling has to leave. Fall is almost over and the color of the leaves on the trees and the color of the sky indicate that winter is just arriving. Looking at the sky, the Ugly Duckling is surprised to see a group of big white birds, with shiny feathers and long flexible necks, flying gracefully toward warmer lands where they would spend the winter.

Ugly Duckling:
> "Winter is near. I will have to find a place for shelter and do my best to wait for the arrival of the spring."

Narrator:
The little duck wakes up one day and realizes that spring has come.

Ugly Duckling:
"Oh, these flowers smell so good, and the grass is so green and the sky is so blue..."

Narrator:
The duck looks up at the sky and again sees the same white birds with long necks coming back from their winter trip.

Ugly Duckling:
"What beautiful birds! I would give anything to be like them!"

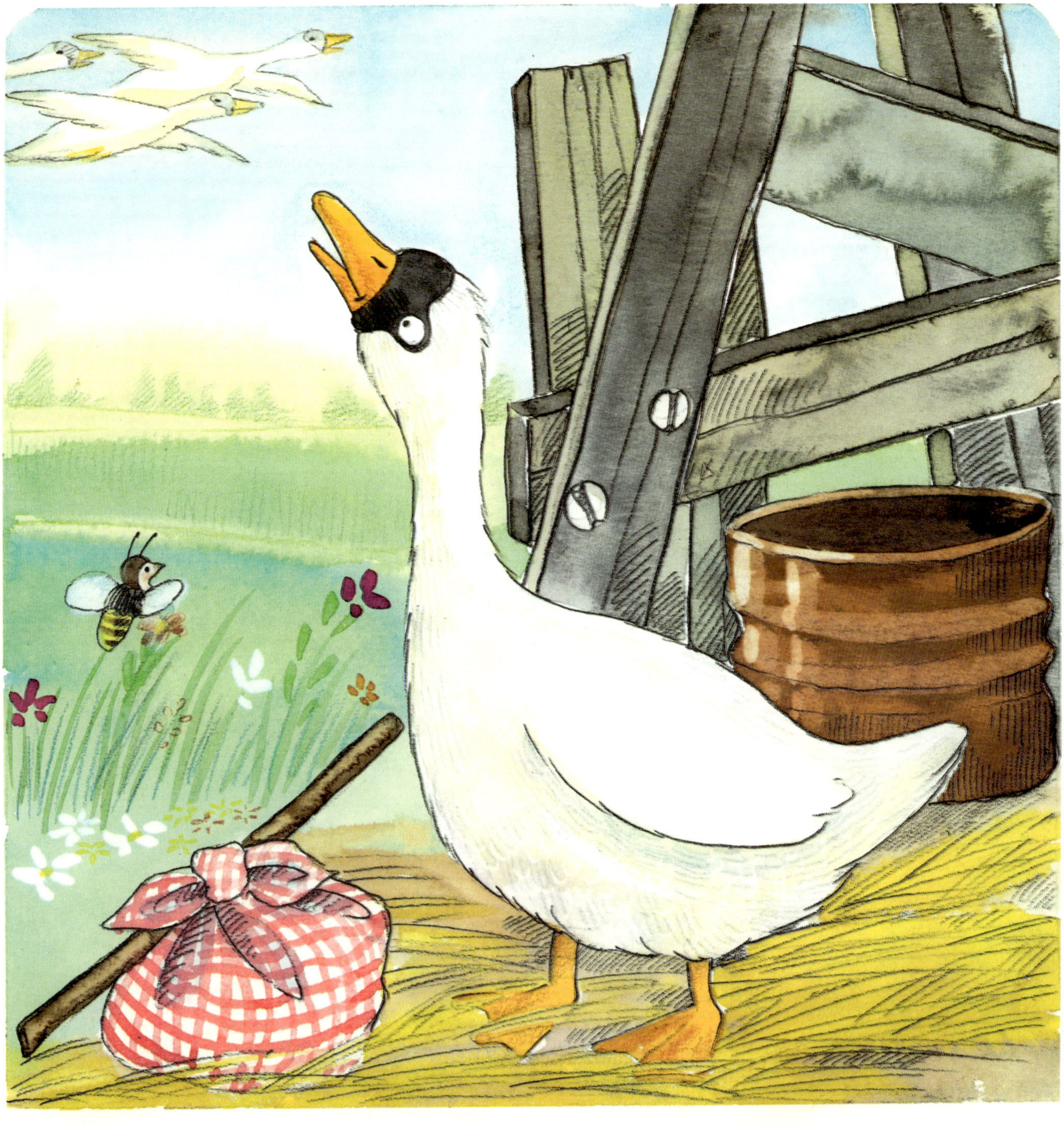

Swans:
"Hello, Brother! What are you doing here, all alone?"

Ugly Duckling: *(Surprised)*
"Me, your brother? Are you kidding me? I am just an ordinary, ugly bird..."

Swans:
"How can you say that? Get closer to the water and look at your reflection."

Ugly Duckling: *(Gets closer to the water and sees his figure reflected there)*
"But... it is not possible! I am big, majestic, and white! My neck is like yours—long and elegant!"

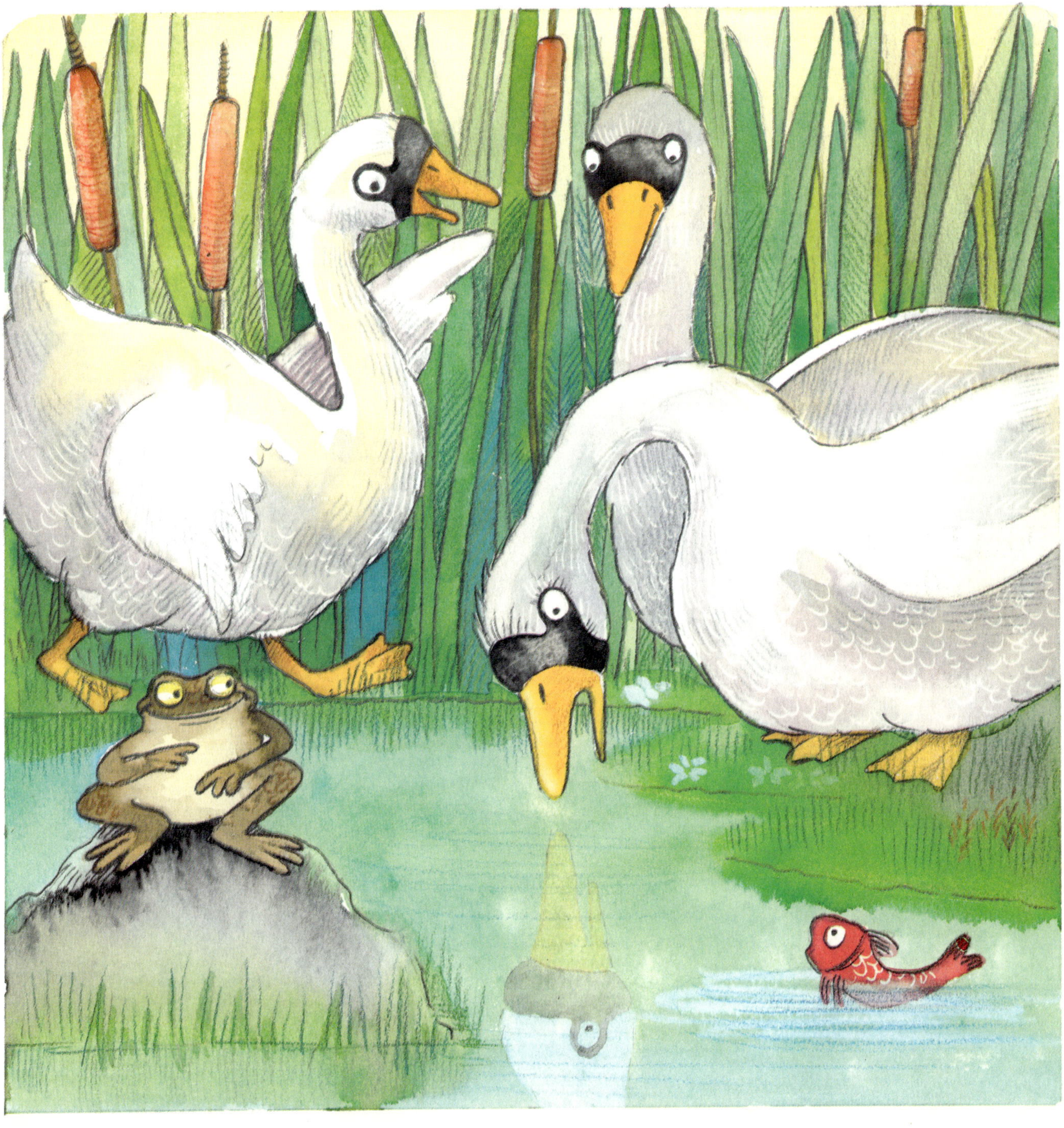

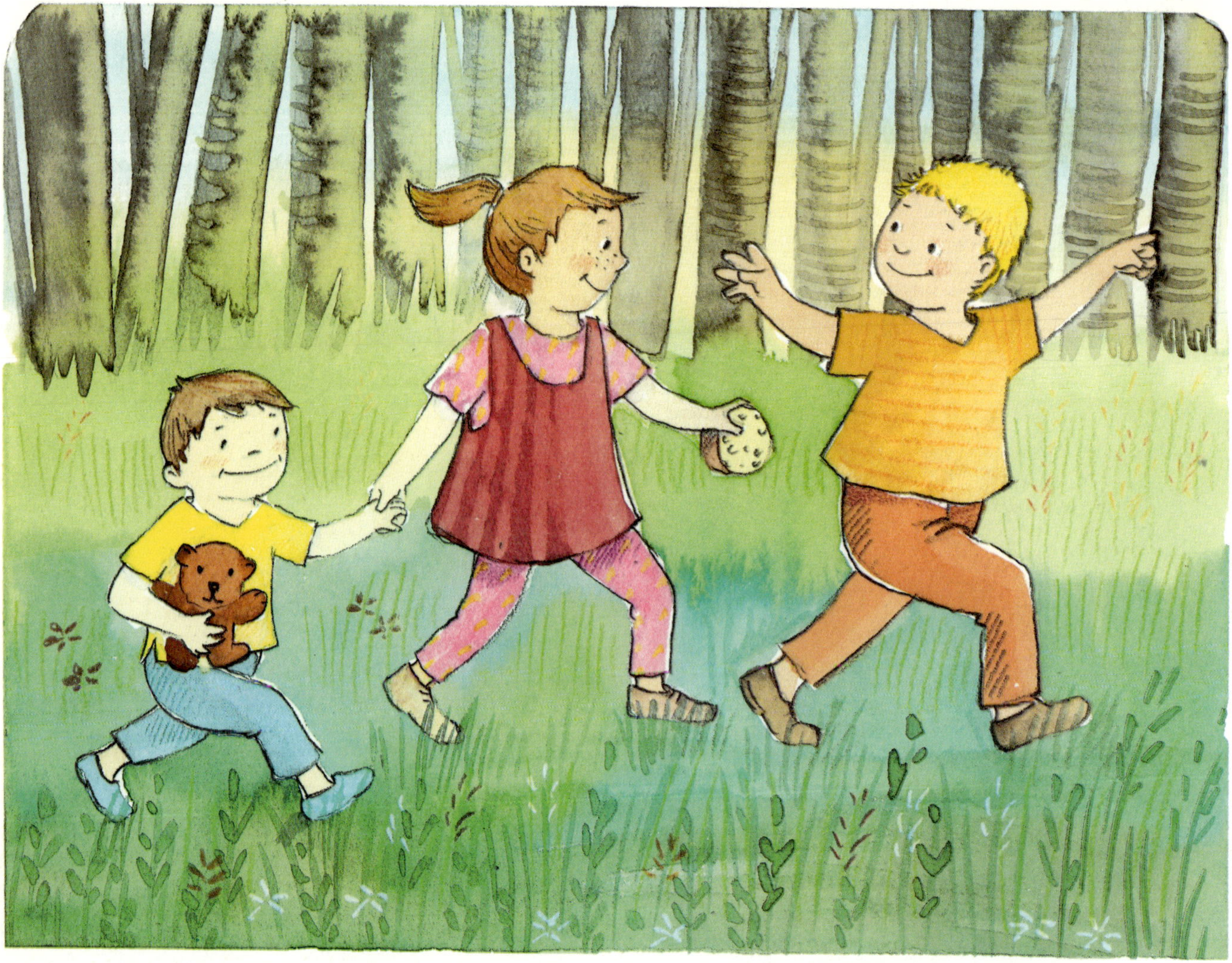

(Some children appear laughing and shouting)

First Boy:

"Look, look! We have found the swans!"

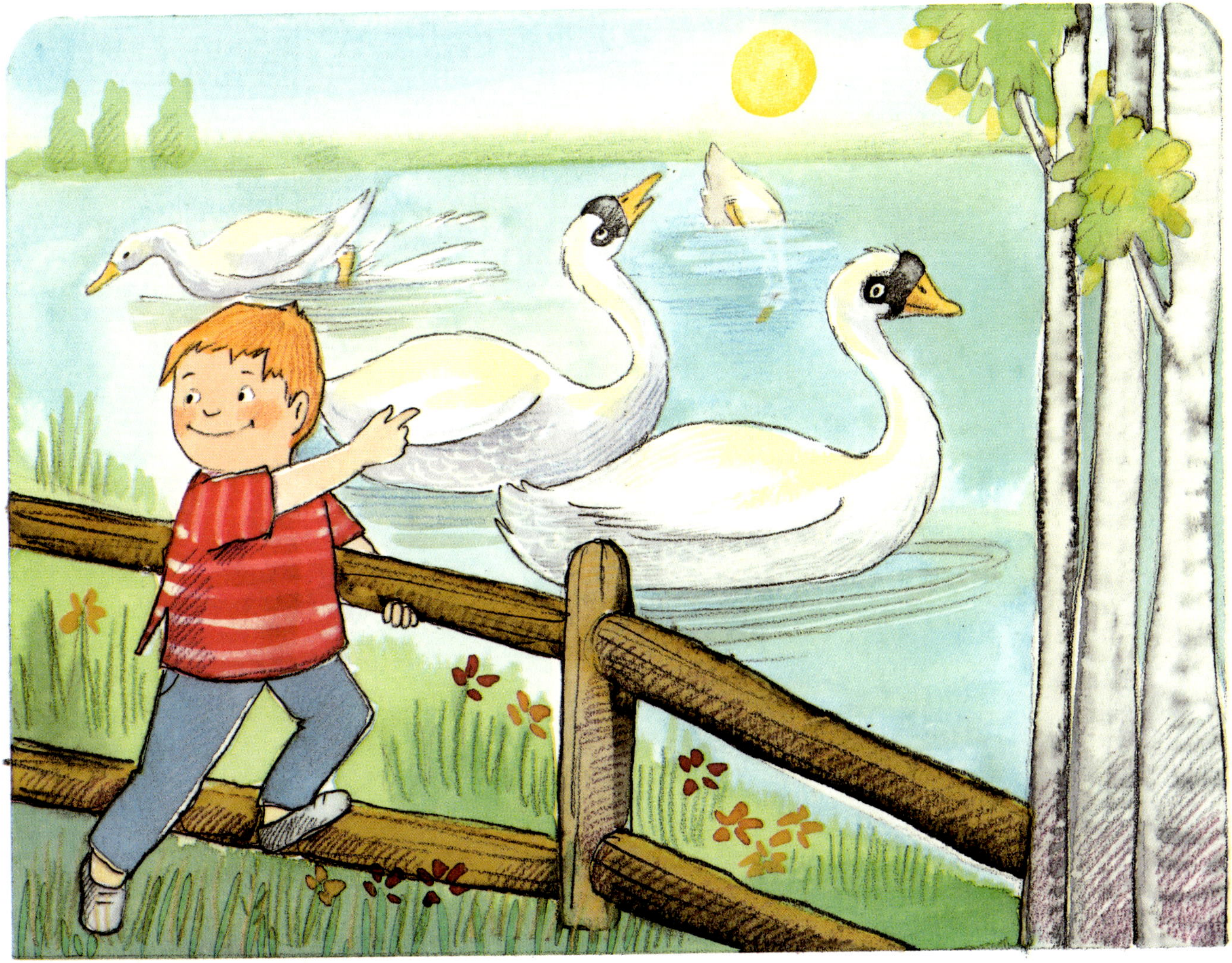

Second Boy:

"Yes, and there is a new one. It seems to be the youngest of all."

Girl:

"It is the most beautiful swan in all the lake. Let's give them some bread crumbs..."

Ugly Duckling: *(Amazed and talking to himself)*
"I am a swan! I have lived all those days of bitterness and loneliness, but now I know who I am and I also know I will never be alone again. *(Talking to the other swans)* If I am a swan, will I be able to fly like you when fall comes again?"

Swans:
"Of course you will. Now, come swim with us and we will introduce you to the rest of the family."

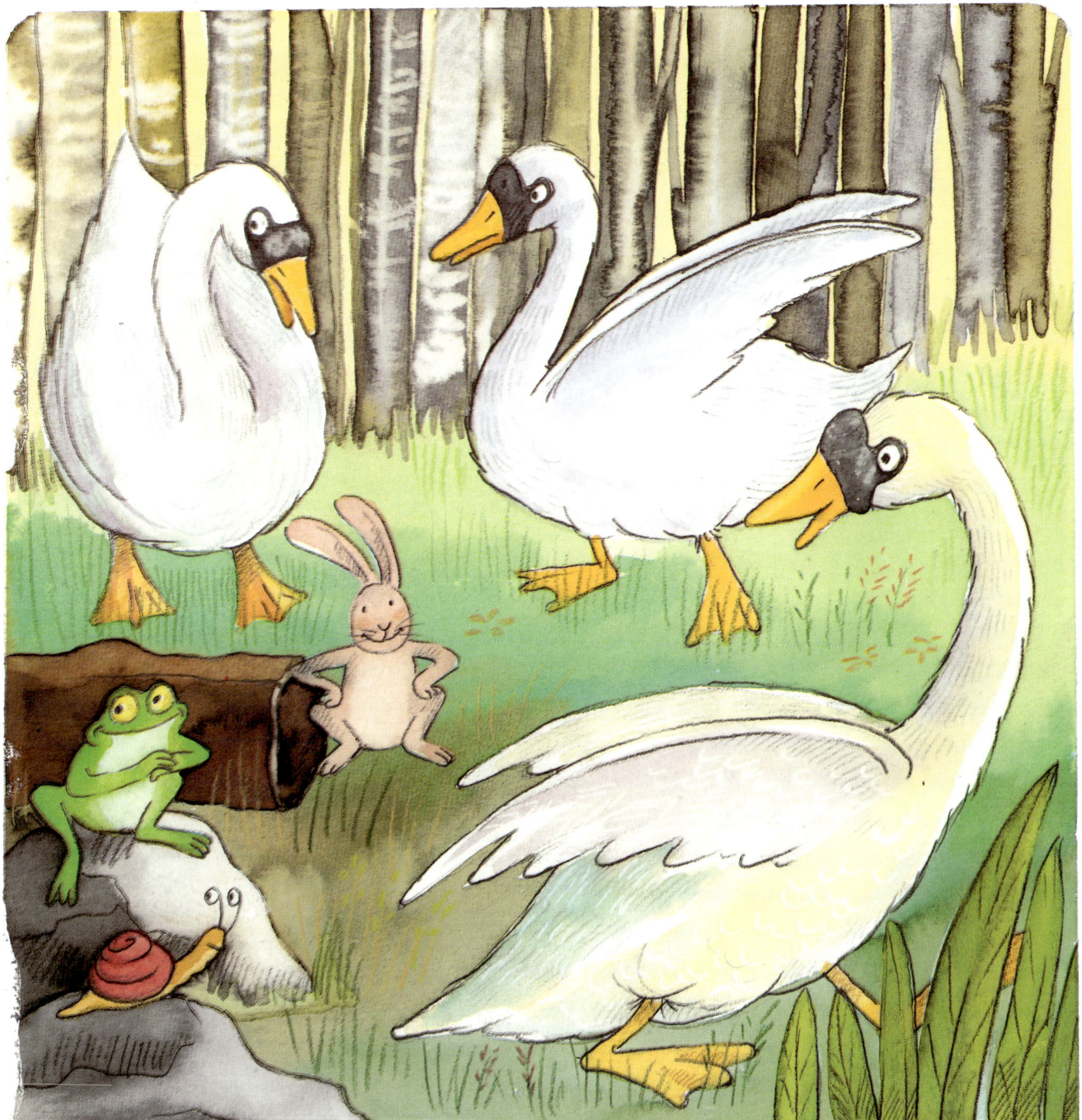

Narrator:
With this change from an Ugly Duckling into a beautiful swan, our hero is able to forget the sad times spent at the farm, the bad treatment by the hen and the cat, and the days of sorrow and loneliness. Now it is like the other swans, and it enjoys its new life, gliding elegantly and smoothly on the lake.

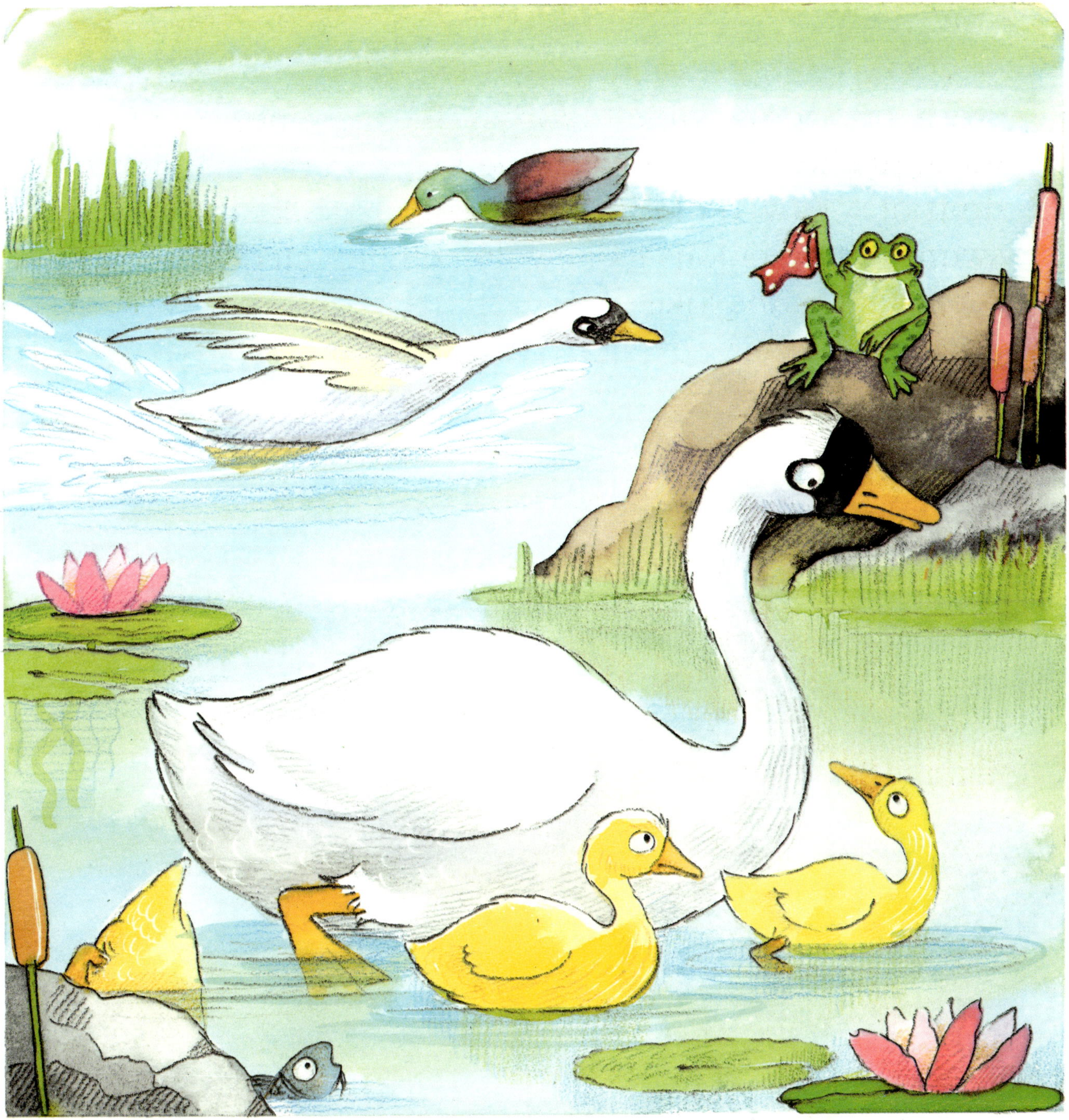

ACTIVITIES

Some of the activities related to this play can include the following:

1. Making animal sounds. Separate the children into groups of two or three. Assign each group an animal that they must try to imitate. Blindfold the children and then separate each group. While the children imitate the noises made by their assigned animal, have each child try to rejoin his group by listening to the various animal sounds.

2. Getting to know animals. Have the children draw different animals on pieces of construction paper. Animals can include chickens, pigs, bears, lions, etc. Cut each animal out and paste to a larger drawing of each animal's natural habitat.

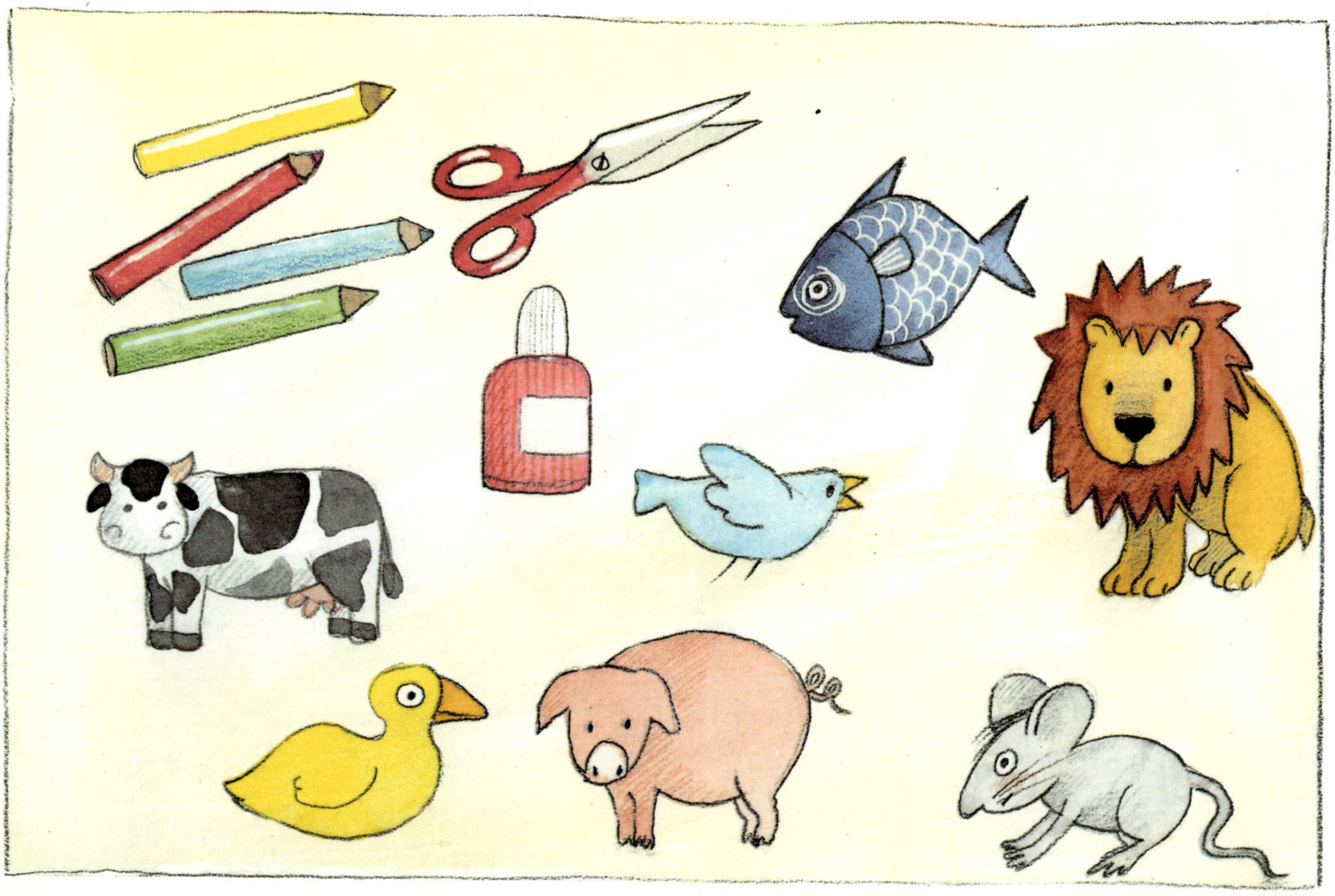

3. Making a weather calendar. Construct a calendar by choosing one or two weeks from each of the four seasons: winter, spring, summer, and fall. Using a large piece of construction paper, draw the lines of a calendar. Then assign the different days of the week to each box. Use different symbols to indicate the types of weather seen in each season, such as rain, sun, snow, and clouds.

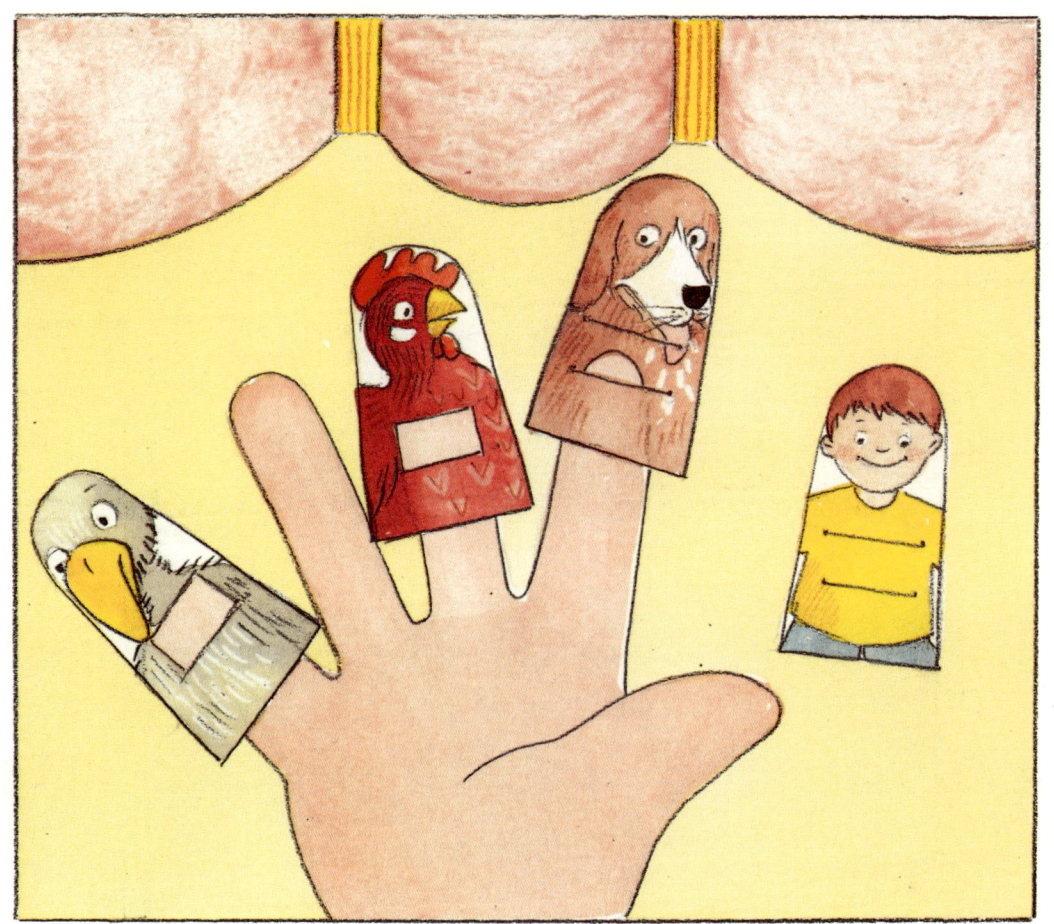

4. Another activity consists of making very simple finger puppets. Cut out each character shown in the illustration and paste onto cardboard. Make the two cuts indicated in the drawing.

Place the puppets on your fingers and act out the story.

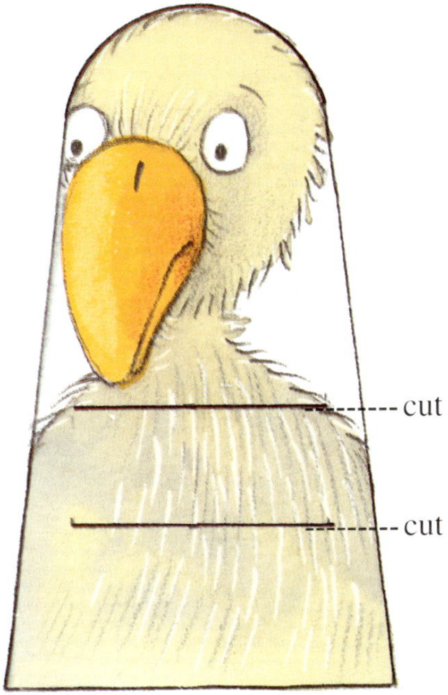
cut
cut

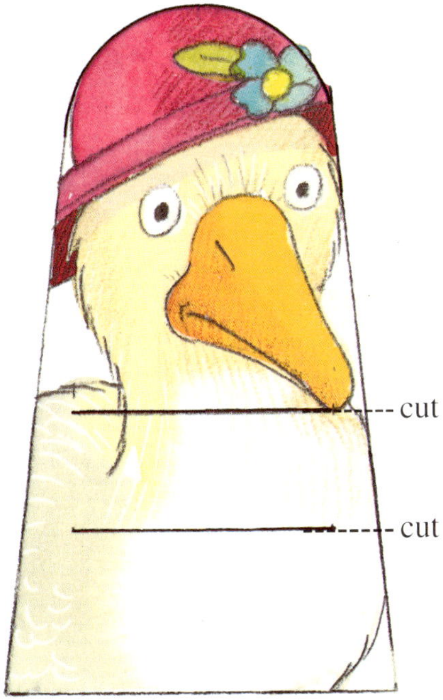
cut
cut

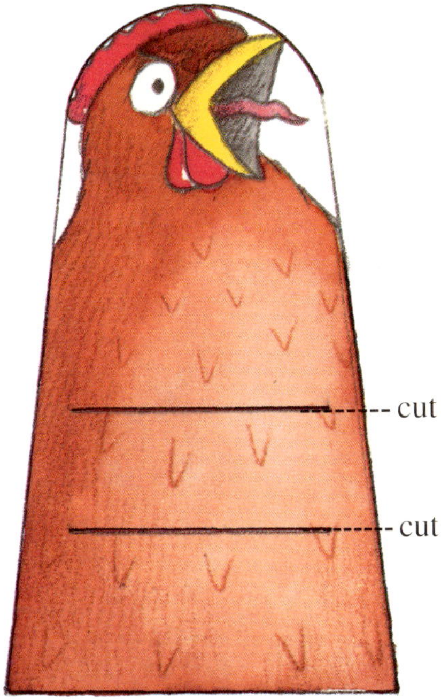
cut
cut

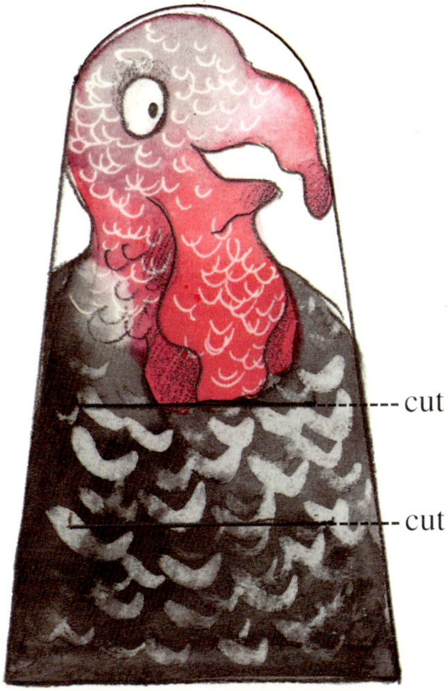
cut
cut

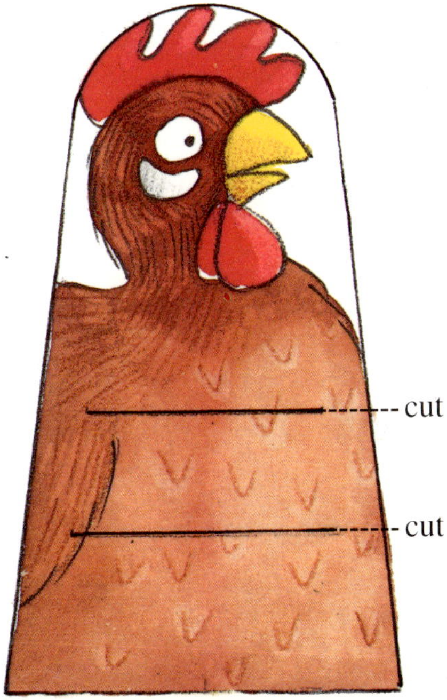
cut
cut

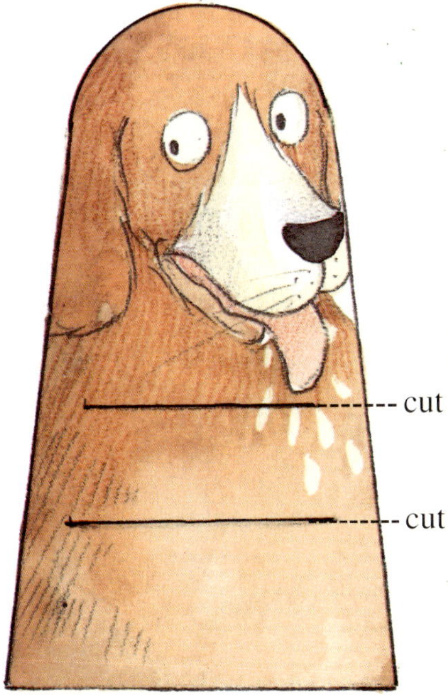
cut
cut

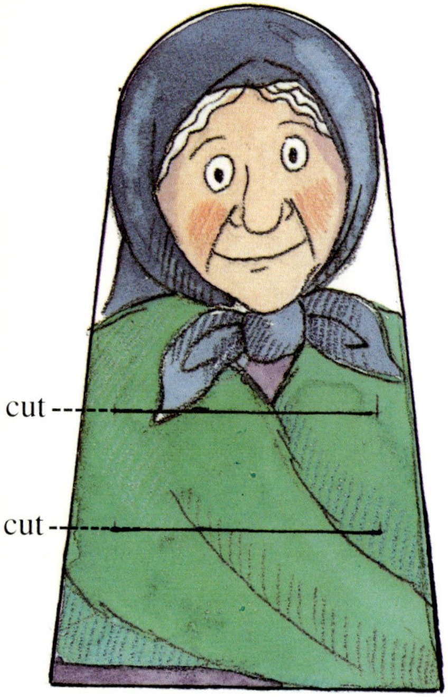
cut
cut

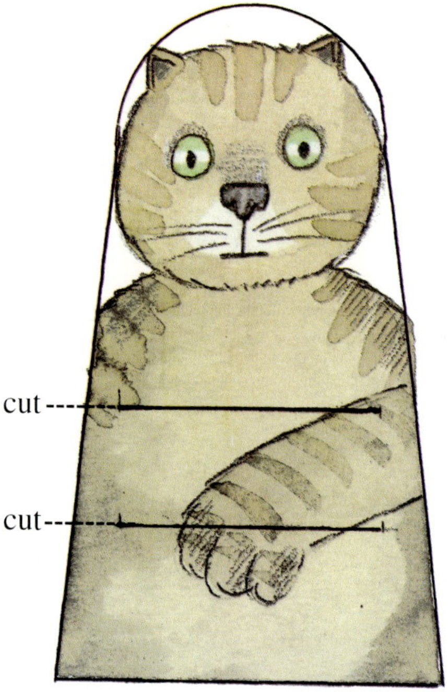
cut
cut

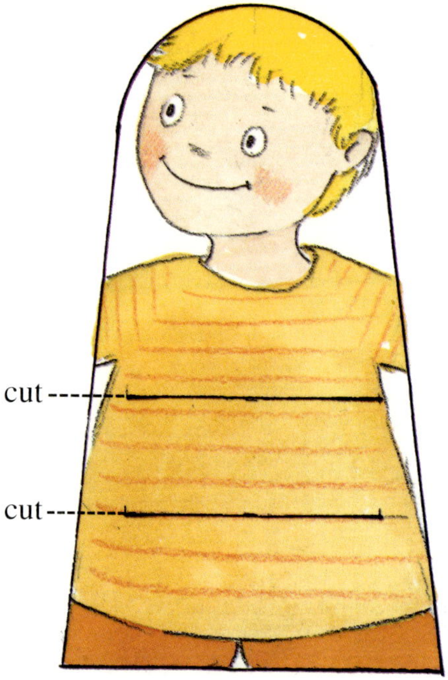
cut
cut

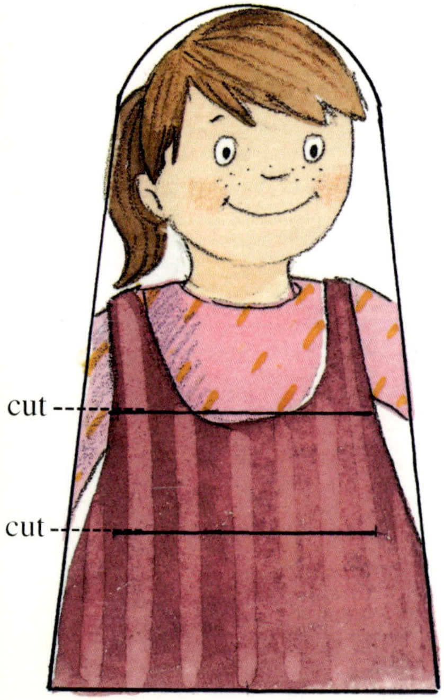
cut
cut

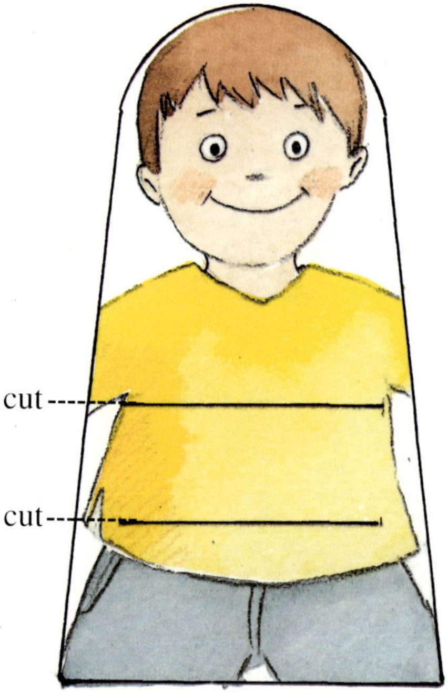
cut
cut

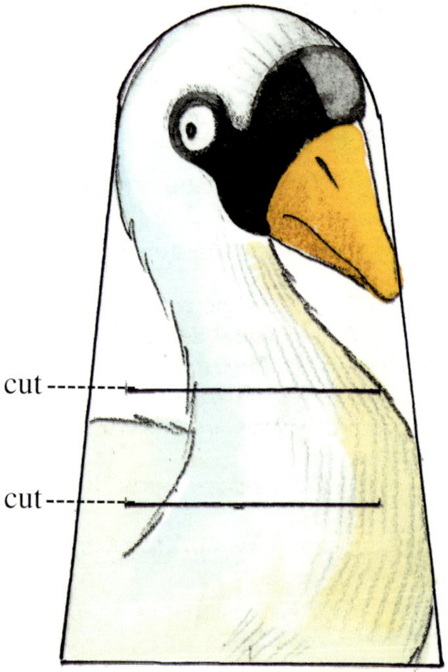
cut
cut

English language version published by Barron's Educational Series, Inc., 1999

Original title of the book in Catalan:
L' ANEGUET LLEIG
One in the series *Teatre dels contes*
Illustrations by Carme Peris
Adapted by Mónica Bosom
Design by Carme Peris

Copyright © TREVOL PRODUCCIONS EDITORIALS, S.C.P., 1999. Barcelona, Spain.

All rights reserved.

No part of this book may be reproduced in any form, by photostat, microfilm, xerography, or any other means, or incorporated into any information retrieval system, electronic or mechanical, without the written permission of the copyright owner.

All inquiries should be addressed to:
Barron's Educational Series, Inc.
250 Wireless Boulevard
Hauppauge, New York 11788
http://www.barronseduc.com

International Standard Book No. 0-7641-5149-5

Library of Congress Catalog Card No. 98-73633

Printed in Spain
9 8 7 6 5 4 3 2 1